Out There

Out There

Seaerra Miller

LB INK

Little, Brown and Company

New York Boston

About This Book

This book was edited by Andrea Colvin and designed by Carolyn Bull.
The production was supervised by Bernadette Flinn, and the production editor was Jake Regier.
The text was set in Seaerra Font 3.

Little, Brown Ink
Hachette Book Group
1290 Avenue of the Americas, New York, NY 10104
Visit us at LBYR.com

First Edition: June 2023

Little, Brown Ink is an imprint of Little, Brown and Company.
The Little, Brown Ink name and logo are trademarks of Hachette Book Group, Inc.

The publisher is not responsible for websites (or their content)
that are not owned by the publisher.

Little, Brown and Company books may be purchased in bulk for business,
educational, or promotional use. For information, please contact your local bookseller
or the Hachette Book Group Special Markets Department at special.markets@hbgusa.com.

Library of Congress Cataloging-in-Publication Data
Names: Miller, Seaerra, author, illustrator.
Title: Out there / Seaerra Miller.
Description: First edition. | New York : Little, Brown and Company, 2023. | Audience: Ages 8–12. | Summary: "Julia goes on a self-discovery-filled road trip with her UFO-obsessed father to chase a meteor shower." —Provided by publisher.
Identifiers: LCCN 2022031420 | ISBN 9780316591867 (hardcover) | ISBN 9780316591874 (trade paperback) | ISBN 9780316591850 (ebook)
Subjects: CYAC: Graphic novels. | Fathers and daughters—Fiction.
Unidentified flying objects—Fiction. | Friendship—Fiction. | LCGFT: Graphic novels.
Classification: LCC PZ7.7.M5528 Ou 2023 | DDC 741.5/973—dc23/eng/20220726
LC record available at https://lccn.loc.gov/2022031420

ISBNs: 978-0-316-59186-7 (hardcover), 978-0-316-59187-4 (pbk.), 978-0-316-59185-0 (ebook),
978-0-316-34423-4 (ebook), 978-0-316-34433-3 (ebook)

PRINTED IN CHINA

1010

Hardcover: 10 9 8 7 6 5 4 3 2 1

Paperback: 10 9 8 7 6 5 4 3 2 1

Are you sure you don't wanna come in? It's really shallow right here. I can touch on my tiptoes.

I'm fine.

That thing at Macinsey's pool party was like three years ago.

I almost drowned!

Yeah, but Brad Perry pulled you out, and that in itself should make the whole thing a really good memory. Tell me again about how soft his skin was...

No way, not again, Sara!

Fine, whatever.

So did you say no to the Hawaii trip with me because of the water phobia situation?

No, it's not that... You know how important this New Mexico trip is to me and my dad...

I just don't understand why you can't move the date around? It's not like the hot, boring old desert is going anywhere.

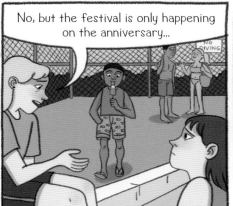

No, but the festival is only happening on the anniversary...

What festival?

Hey, Sean! Julia's going to some alien convention with her dad. A bunch of people are going to the desert where they think some spaceship crashed like a hundred years ago.

Seventy-five years ago.

What? Like, just in the middle of the desert?

Kind of. It's a town in the desert called Roswell. In the '40s they found a bunch of debris there from something that crashed. Some people think it was a UFO.

Whoa, seriously?

Yeah. It's actually pretty cool. They have this big festival every year with people who study UFOs and stuff.

Julia's dad is, like, way into that stuff.

Oh yeah, isn't your dad that guy who always wears that weird alien shirt?

Um, yeah.

He, like, thinks aliens took him into their spaceship.

Ha! What?!

Sara! What the heck?

Sorry! I thought, like, since you're going on this trip, you were telling people.

HONK!

Jules! I'm here!

Is that your mom?

Yeah.

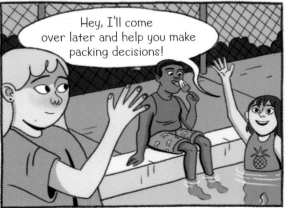

Hey, I'll come over later and help you make packing decisions!

OK, which dress should you take? This one totally matches your eyes, but this one doesn't have sleeves, so you won't get sweat stains from the gross desert heat...

He did not have a breakdown. My dad wouldn't make this up...

I'm just saying your dad, whether he was abducted by aliens or not, hasn't been the best dad lately. He always says y'all are going to go do something, and then he is, like, super late or doesn't show up...

He has a lot going on. Look, I don't want to fight with you about this.

I'm not trying to fight with you.

This trip is different. It's really important to both of us. We are gonna listen to the Beatles and sing really badly and drink all the soda my mom never lets me have, and it's gonna be amazing.

OK, OK. I get it, but you have to text me and tell me if you find, like, a crashed spaceship or something.

It's seriously gonna just be, like, people who study UFOs and researchers and stuff like that.

Sounds so much cooler than Hawaii with your best friend...

Sara...

All right, it's just that I'm gonna miss you.

Me too.

Now, let's pick out a pair of cute shoes just in case...

He's so late.

He's always late.

When people are late it means they don't value your time.

That's not true. Dad's brain is just distracted.

Look, the waiter is giving us the stink eye because we've been sitting here so long.

I think that's just his face. Look, here's Dad!

Am I late?!

Only by 20 minutes or so.

Sorry, Emily. I was finishing some last-minute stuff before we take off tomorrow.

I hope that includes taking the car to the mechanic. I thought I saw smoke coming out of it when you picked up Julia last weekend.

Pssh...Ruby is the most reliable transport around! She's a firecracker.

Except in the morning, of course, and at night, and if we have an especially stinky snack.

We'll just have a large pepperoni pizza, please.

I've got everything covered. I promise.

Yeah, Mom. Dad's got it covered. Stop worrying!

But it's what I do best.

It's only three days.

I got you a little something for the ride.

Dad! No way! This is Sig Bell's new book! I've been dying to read this!

Thank you!

Of course. You are a budding UFOlogist, after all.

SIGH

OK, all cozy? You need anything? Extra pillow? Milk? Oh, wait, I don't think I have milk. Um, water?

I'm fine, Dad.

Roswell is the site of the most famous UFO incident in the world. It is a story that begins in 1947 in a sleepy little New Mexico town and ends with government conspiracies, mysterious technologies, and most important, the possibility of life beyond this earth.

What was it that crashed in the desert that night in 1947? Was the mysterious craft brought down by electrical storms in the area, and why did the air force engage in a

Journey with me as we talk to the rancher who stumbled upon the site before it was altered and meet, for the very first time, an eyewi~~ whose testimony sheds~~ light on the most intrig~~ question of all: What or w~~ was inside that craft?

cover-up, replacing the wreckage with debris from a weather balloon?

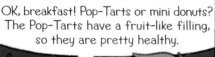
OK, breakfast! Pop-Tarts or mini donuts? The Pop-Tarts have a fruit-like filling, so they are pretty healthy.

No fruit for me! Donuts.

That's my kid! OK, one more thing and we can go.

You told Mom you fixed the car...

It just needs a little extra go-juice once in a while, and we might not be able to run the air-conditioning, but we'll acclimate! Ruby is solid.

All right, kid. What are you doing just standing there? We gotta go! Everybody is waiting on you!

I know you think you're funny...

Luckily, so does everyone else.

All right! Here we go!

Yes!

Julia.

Huh?

Look.

Some rocks?

No, look! It's a camel. See, that's the head.

Right...

Cool, huh?! Like it drank a big lake or something and settled down for a nap.

Yeah, Dad.

Wow, it looks so different out here. It's so...empty.

OK, I wanna get a picture of you with the camel.

Dad!

Come on, these are memories!

OK, but, like, don't do it from a weird angle.

I'll do it from a very normal and boring angle. Come on!

Got it.

Here. I'll send it to you so you can post it on your social medias.

All right, back in the car. We're on a schedule here!

All right, Ruby. I hear you.

VRRRRRR

Gotta fill her with some coolant.

On the road again.

It looks like an alien planet out there.

In what way?

I don't know. There's just, like, nothing out there. Like those pictures of Mars. And plus, the moon is out but it's daytime, like in *Star Wars*.

We are space explorers out in our little Ruby Rover, collecting scientific data like how long two people can survive on Twinkies and which gas station in New Mexico has the stinkiest bathroom!

Important information!

Communication link from planet Earth!

Hi, Mom.

We are on the road! No, Dad's not driving too fast! Yes, I have my seat belt on! For breakfast? We had fruit. Yep, I'll text you when we get there, I promise. OK, Mom. OK. Love you, too.

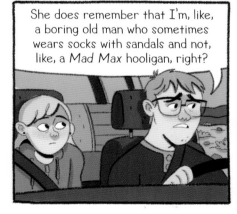

She does remember that I'm, like, a boring old man who sometimes wears socks with sandals and not, like, a *Mad Max* hooligan, right?

She knows. She's just Mom.

Yeah. I think she's called me 50 times in the last week.

Honestly, I thought she might be hiding in my suitcase. She's so uptight sometimes. Do you think she's always been like that?

No. Not when we first met.

Really? How did y'all meet?

She came to one of my gigs, and as soon as she saw me shredding on the guitar, she was instantly in love with me.

Mm-hmm. Sure, Dad.

Yep. She couldn't resist my sick guitar solos.

Oh my gosh.

She was a bit of a wild child. She'd crowd-surf at all my shows. Sometimes she'd call me at midnight to go for a drive, just to drink milkshakes and listen to music...

I wish she did stuff like that now.

She loves you so much. She just wants to make sure you're OK.

Yeah, but sometimes it's too much. She wasn't like this when you were home.

I wish you were still living with us.

I know.

I just don't think it's fair that Mom made you go. Like, she won't even try to get it.

Get what?

The UFO stuff!

Julia...

I mean, how could she not believe you?

It's not an easy thing to believe if you didn't experience it.

Yeah, but you always believe the people who you love.

I wish it were that simple, kiddo.

I know what we need.

This is Sig Bell Bizarre America coming to you live! Today on the show we've got an exciting lineup! First, I wanna give a shout-out to all you Bizarros who are headed to Roswell this weekend for the 75th anniversary of the Roswell crash!

EEEEE! That's us!

Keep your eyes to the skies! There's a big meteor shower happening at the same time as the event. Coincidence? Perhaps not!

Wow.

Whoa.

Right?

This is so cool! Look, there's the old police station where Jesse Marcel took the UFO wreckage!

POLICE DEPT

Super cool!

Come on, Josh, smile!

OK, one more.

Smile!

Not fair!

MOM

Made it

ROSWELL

55

Do you think the aliens are up there? Right now?

No, not yet.

How do you know?

Just a feeling.

HOWL

What was that?!

Just the coyotes. Should we talk to them?

Talk to them?

Yeah. Here, listen.

OK, OK.

Did you hear that?!

Now, if my translation is correct, they say we are welcome to stay, but we have to make our beds in the morning and keep the snoring to a minimum.

All right, wild animal, bedtime!

Night, kiddo.

Night, Dad.

Wait, does that screw on there? No, over here.

Is everything OK with Ruby?

Just tightening things up, ya know? Lug nuts, pistons, car stuff.

Do you know what you're doing?

Duh, I'm a dad.

What's for breakfast?

Check the cooler in the back.

She can kinda be a butt sometimes, huh?

Dad!

What?

I just think sometimes she doesn't...you know... get me. Like, she glosses over the parts of me she doesn't like.

Trust me, kid. I know exactly how that feels.

Really?

Um, people aren't usually super excited to hear that I was abducted by aliens who told me they're gonna give me a super-important, life-changing message.

All right, then, let the UFOing commence.

Wow, there's a ton to do--a parade, a showing of *The Day the Earth Stood Still*, and, oh, look. This is cool--an abductee meetup! Where should we start?

Awesome.

Kecksburg, PA
1965

KENTUCKY   MISSISSIPPI   WEST VIRGINIA

AREA
51

ROSWELL
CRASH
JULY 8, 1947

Picture time.

Huh,
huh.

CLICK

Whoa...

This is it. This is exactly what they looked like. Well, I mean, of course the craft was a little bigger and the backdrop was our backyard, but they nailed the lights.

Really?

I do think they only had four fingers, though, not five.

Hmmm...

Maybe we should check out the big exhibit.

Lead the way!

...OST DEBRIS FOUND

...idden from the public ...or over 50 years, new ...mnants of the Roswell ...JFO have been recovered.

Dad! This is amazing! Oh my gosh!

Dad?

Do you think that was, like, the real deal? Like really from the spaceship?

Definitely! It had the same markings Jesse Marcel described seeing on the debris he found.

You didn't think it kinda looked like...tinfoil?

I mean, there are only so many elements in the universe. It makes sense that alien stuff would look similar to ours.

Julia--

Yes or no?

Yes! Definitely yes!

I WANT TO BELIEVE

ROSWELL INCIDENT

UFO ROS

And look!

For your tie collection! You have to have it!

Oh, man. I threw out my tie collection after I stopped working the ol' nine-to-five office job, but that is pretty fly.

You threw out your ties? But Mom and I gave those to you.

Didn't have room in the new apartment. Sorry, kid. Oh, but look!

You gotta have it!

It looks OK?

It was made for you.

Thanks, Dad!

Hey, I think we can still make it to the alien-abduction group. Let's scoot and skedaddle!

That museum was kinda full of normies, but I think these are gonna be our people.

Come on, gather 'round. We are all friends here!

END UAP SECRECY

Welcome, all! It's wonderful to see so many brothers and sisters here today to celebrate our shared experience as contactees.

This group is really about exploring our gift from the beings above. My name is Clarabella.

Let's go around the circle and all say our names.

Jeff.

Annie.

Aubrey.

Julia.

David.

Carol.

Greg.

END UAP SECREC

So lovely to meet you all. Just wonderful. So, who wants to share with the group?

Go ahead.

They've been abducting me since childhood. It used to scare me so much, but lately I've found a way to work through it.

Art has helped me process the experience.

The thing is, I have a special connection with the UFOs. I've seen dozens upon dozens of them. Orbs, saucers, triangles.

I'll just be looking out my front window in the morning, having a cup of coffee, and there will be one hovering in the distance. I can sense them, too.

I'll be at work, and the hair on the back of my neck will stand up, or it'll feel like my teeth are buzzing, and I'll look up, and there one will be.

I can feel them above us right now.

Course they
are invisible.

Of course. Um,
does anyone else have a
story they'd like to
share?

How about you?

Um...

All right.

Well...

It happened a few years ago, and, well...

I guess it started off as a pretty normal day.

"It was a Saturday, so I was home. It'd been a terrible week at work, and I was exhausted. But as the day progressed, I felt something more than that.

"Something was off. Everything was too still. All day there was no wind, not even a breeze. I didn't hear birds chirping or insects buzzing.

"I was fixated on the feeling, but when I mentioned it to my wife, she thought I was losing it. I was so distracted that I absentmindedly poured bacon grease down the drain and clogged it. My wife and I got into this huge fight. We were fighting a lot back then.

"She was so mad, and we ended up going to bed without speaking. I couldn't fall asleep, and not just because of the fight. It was too quiet.

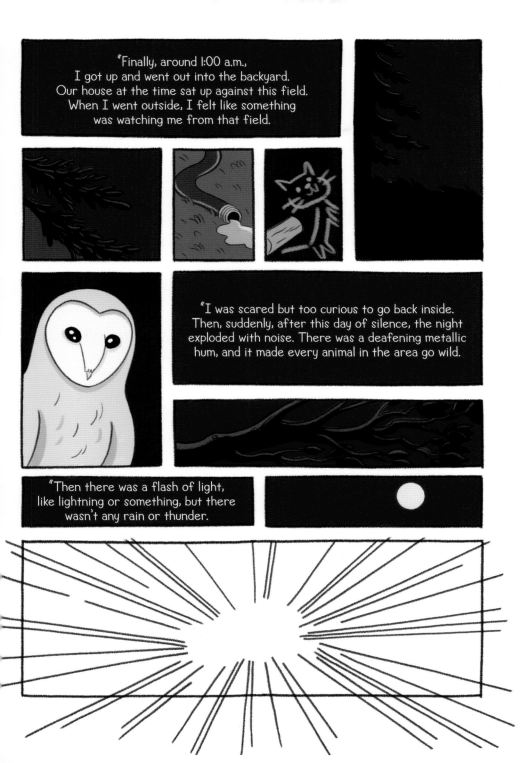

"Finally, around 1:00 a.m.,
I got up and went out into the backyard.
Our house at the time sat up against this field.
When I went outside, I felt like something
was watching me from that field.

"I was scared but too curious to go back inside.
Then, suddenly, after this day of silence, the night
exploded with noise. There was a deafening metallic
hum, and it made every animal in the area go wild.

"Then there was a flash of light,
like lightning or something, but there
wasn't any rain or thunder.

"The next thing I knew, I was...somewhere else. There were stars everywhere. I had never seen so many stars, and I couldn't move.

"I could only look straight ahead, and I was lying flat on my back against something cold and hard. I could see shadowy figures all around me. I wanted to call out to them, but I couldn't speak. Then it was like I just knew that I could talk to them in my head.

"When I did, one of them stepped into view. Its eyes were huge and black, but I wasn't scared. I knew it wasn't going to hurt me. More of them came forward.

"They were all talking at once inside my head, but not with words--with pictures. Even though they were talking simultaneously, I could understand each of them perfectly.

"They were telling me something important, somewhere I had to be.

"They had a message for me,
but it wasn't the right time.

"I had to find them,
find the place they
had shown me.

"I don't remember much else before waking up on a lawn chair in the backyard.

"I sat there the rest of the night, trying to understand what had just happened to me.

"When the sun rose, I went back to bed. My wife was still fast asleep, totally unaware of what had just happened to me, but I knew I was completely changed."

I've been searching ever since, trying to find where they were telling me to go. I've studied star maps and researched the type of vegetation I saw and where it grows--

and I have finally figured it out.

The meteor shower...You think the one tomorrow is the one the aliens showed you?

Yes! Exactly!

I bet they are going to tell you where the Reptilian underground base is so you can get a leg up in the secret alien war, or I wonder if they'll share why they built the ancient Egyptian pyramids!

No, wait... I bet it's about the human-alien hybrid program. Has to be.

BZZT

Sara Calling

No! It's the guy who was sitting behind her in the scene where she's in math! She asks if she can borrow his pencil, and he says, "Sorry, I've only got a pen!"

Um, cool?

Yeah! Super cool, right?! He was eating at the same restaurant as us! That's where we saw that alien statue I sent you the picture of...

You know that's not what aliens actually look like, though, right?

So?

I just mean, like, that's not what the aliens that took my dad look like.

Why are you being so weird? It was just a joke.

OK, well, I have to go, actually.

Seriously? I just called!

Yeah, my dad is motioning to get going.

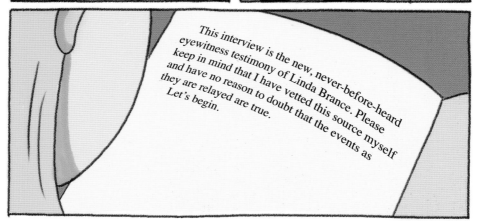

This interview is the new, never-before-heard eyewitness testimony of Linda Brance. Please keep in mind that I have vetted this source myself and have no reason to doubt that the events as they are relayed are true.
Let's begin.

"I grew up on a 50-acre sheep ranch just outside of Roswell. I lived with my parents and two younger brothers. Lots of desert out that way and nothing much to fill it."

Can you walk us through what happened that day, before you saw the crash?

"It was July, which meant the sheep were out to pasture and there wasn't much work to be done around the farm. I'd spent the day helping my mother do laundry and watching a big afternoon thunderstorm roll in across the prairie.

"It was nearly dark when the rain started. My father sent me up to the top pasture to make sure the sheep could get to higher ground.

"Sometimes those low basins fill up with water and turn into rivers when the ground is hard and dry.

"I was soaked through by the time I made it to the gate.

"I was ready to turn around and run home, when I noticed something."

Hey, kiddo. You ran off.

Yeah, sorry. Sara called.

Greg and Carol invited us over for dinner.

Hi.

And this is their son, Josh.

Hey.

Hi.

CHAPTER 4

How great is this?!

It's really cool.

Head in. I'll give you the grand tour.

Home away from home! We travel to all the UFO conventions and festivals and eventually decided we want to do it in style!

It's fantastic!

Well, we like it. Josh, why don't you go show Julia your game while I make dinner.

Fine.

Wait, take this. It's getting chilly out there!

What are you playing?

Alien Terminator.

Cool.

So...you've been to Roswell before?

Every year.

Really? That's so awesome. I think it's beautiful, like, the desert and everything. Plus, like, the town is so cool.

Sure. If you say so.

So...you've been abducted by aliens?

What?!

I just thought 'cause you were at the meetup thing...

No. No way.

My parents have some delusion that they were. They drag me to all sorts of these stupid things.

Sorry. I just assumed...

What about you? You were at the meeting. Were you "taken"?

No. Just my dad.

Trust me, all these people are full of it. No offense or anything, but they all just want attention or something, or to, like, be special, I guess.

My dad is special.

You really think aliens came from like a billion trillion miles away, looked all over Earth just to find your dad standing in the backyard in his underwear, and thought they'd, like, take him to space, just for kicks?

They're from Zeta Reticuli, which is only 39 light-years from Earth.

Seriously? Do you hear yourself? Your dad is just as full of it as the rest of them.

You don't even know him.

Whatever.

You travel all over to all these UFO conventions, and, like, you really don't believe any of it's real?! What about Rendlesham Forest or the Phoenix Lights?

I'm not saying that people don't see lights in the sky or some weird stuff. I'm saying my parents do this not because aliens kidnapped them, but because it makes them feel important.

It is important.

You've clearly been brainwashed.

I just don't see how you can't believe!

And why exactly should I believe? Does your dad have some kind of proof? How do you know he's telling the truth?

Because he's my dad... He wouldn't lie to me.

Parents lie all the time.

My dad doesn't.

Whatever.

"I could see a pink glow just over the horizon, and I began to walk toward it.

"I stumbled around in the dark, tripping over rocks and brush, until I got to the bottom of a hill. I could tell that whatever it was was just on the other side. I started to climb, but something stopped me.

"There was this giant metallic disk crashed into the side of the arroyo, surrounded by pieces of jagged and broken metal. There were men from the air force base everywhere. They reminded me of ants, crawling all over the desert, collecting pieces of debris, and they were taking pictures and such. Then I noticed some of them were standing over something.

"I risked getting closer to see what they were looking at. To this day, I wonder if I'd have been a happier person if I didn't see that thing on the ground."

Do you remember that time they took us when we were up driving through Oregon?

Must've been gone at least six hours that time.

Do you remember any of what happened during that missing time?

Oh, definitely.

They were collecting all sorts of things from us--hair, fingernail clippings...

I swear one of 'em was trying to pull my tooth out!

And they had these little metal instruments they used to scrape skin samples.

That's so wild! They did that to me, too!

You never told me that before, Dad.

What? Sure I have. Look...

Always studying us. You'd think at this point it'd be more useful to just sit us down and have a cuppa coffee and a conversation than it would to keep strapping us to metal tables and sniffing our armpits.

They're so advanced, it's hard to say what they are really doing.

Well, maybe David's gonna find that out tomorrow.

I feel like I've just been consumed with wondering why. Why me? Like, I can't focus on anything else. I just need to know, ya know?

It takes over your life.

Something like that.

And what about your mom, Julia? Didn't she come with you two?

Oh, she's home in Colorado.

Emily and I split up a few years ago.

I'm sorry to hear that.

135

What are you doing?

Just looking.

For what?

Why aren't you down at the water?

'Cause my parents are down there.

Your parents seem really nice.

I guess.

BZZZT

BZZZT

Sara Calling

Who was that?

Just my friend Sara.

So why didn't you answer?

She's in Hawaii right now. She invited me, too, and I couldn't go because of this trip with my dad, and she's, like, kinda being a jerk about it.

Wait. You gave up going to Hawaii to come sit in this dusty desert with your dad?

Yeah. She doesn't get the UFO stuff, either. Actually, y'all would probably get along. She thinks all this is really dumb, too.

Wait, you actually told your friend about the alien-abduction stuff?!

Of course. She's my best friend.

So now, instead of talking to your best friend, you are out here looking for UFO scraps?

Well, we are only a few miles from the crash site...

I don't know, actually.

My parents drag me out here every year, and I hate it. I hate the weird people and the boring museum and the fact that I can't talk about it with any of my friends.

Why can't you talk about it with your friends?

It's just so embarrassing, ya know? I've told all my friends that my parents are scientists who travel around documenting the migratory patterns of dung beetles!

And that's less embarrassing than the alien stuff?

Look, I was eight when I came up with that! Dung beetles are cool when you're in third grade!

141

Maybe that would be easier, just not telling anyone.

I'm not sure...I mean, someday people are gonna find out, and then not only are my parents weirdos, but I've also been lying to all my friends.

Sounds kinda lonely, not being able to talk about your real life.

So you seriously hate everything out here?

Well, this isn't bad.

I'd definitely like it more if it were alien goop, but this is pretty cool, too.

You can keep it if you want.

Thanks.

Everybody that comes here is, like, obsessed with things beyond the earth, ya know? But if they took the time to look, maybe they'd realize there's tons of cool stuff right in front of their faces.

It's like they're missing out on everything!

You mean your parents?

My parents, your dad--
all of them.

Jules...

Come down here!

Did you tell your family?

"I wanted to...When I got home, they were all waiting for me. It seemed like the whole thing had been minutes, but I'd been gone over an hour.

"I opened my mouth to tell them...but I couldn't find the words. I began to think that if I told them about the light and the disk and the little body, they'd think I was out of my mind or lying or something."

I could hardly believe what I saw, so how could I expect them to? So, no, I never told them.

Hey, are you OK?

Can we go now?

Of course.

I think we are gonna head off now. Maybe we'll see you at the parade in a bit?

Sure thing.

Thatta girl, Ruby!

VROOM

What happened back there? I thought we were having fun.

You know I hate water, Dad.

What? You hate water? Since when?!

Since I almost drowned at Macinsey Hawkin's pool party?

You never told me that...

Yes, I did! I remember because Mom came and picked me up and took me to the emergency room and we called you.

What happened?

I slipped and hit my head and swallowed a bunch of water, Dad!

I'm sorry. Are you sure you told me that?

Just forget it.

What do you think? This seems like a good spot? We can park here and walk over to the street. It'll be a good view.

I'm gonna go look around.

Wait, aren't we gonna watch this together?

I just want to go look around, Dad.

We need to leave by seven if we're gonna make it to the spot.

I know.

Julia!

You look totally disgusted to see me.

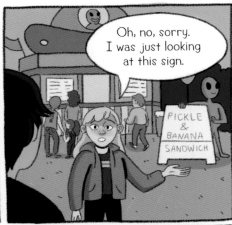

Oh, no, sorry. I was just looking at this sign.

PICKLE & BANANA SANDWICH

We have to try it!

Come on, seriously?

Yes, seriously!

PICKLE & BANANA SANDWICH

It's beautiful.

This smells so good...

Holy smokes! It tastes even better than it smells.

I don't know if that's saying much.

Yum!

So are you OK?

After eating that? No, probably not.

No, I mean you kinda lost it when you thought your dad was gonna throw you into the lake.

I think you were right, maybe. About our parents not seeing what's in front of them sometimes. What if I can't see what's in front of me?

What do you mean?

I mean, I gave up going to Hawaii with my best friend to be here. Was that, like, a huge mistake? I could be, like, drinking out of a coconut right now!

Drinking out of coconuts is overrated.

You know, my dad used to bake and watch old James Bond movies every Saturday night, and he was in a band--and it wasn't, like, boring dad rock, he was actually really good--and he was supposed to teach me to play guitar...

...and then he just wasn't that person anymore. Maybe my mom was right.

You know what Hawaii doesn't have?

Tiny dogs dressed like that.

You know, I found another thing I don't hate about this place.

This fried pickle-banana thing.

I think it's starting!

Wow.

You know, this isn't really what I thought it was gonna be. This festival.

I thought it was gonna be, like, UFO people giving lectures about antigravity hyperdrives, and my dad and me walking through the desert discovering some lost evidence or something.

I know it's dumb. I just thought it was going to be...serious.

I think I should go find my dad.

Oh, OK.

Well, we always stop at that retro diner on the way out of town in the morning. Maybe we'll see you there.

Yeah, that sounds good.

Hey, Dad.

You ready
to go?

Sure.

★ I ★ 👽 ☆
WANT TO ☆
BELIEVE!

★ I ★ 👽 ☆
WANT TO ☆
BELIEVE!

Do you ever miss playing the guitar?

Hmm?

I mean, when I was little, you always played the guitar, and then when the aliens took you, you stopped.

I had bigger things to focus on.

Do you really think we are going to see something tonight?

I know we will.

OK, but, like, how do you know?

What do you mean?

Well, like, Josh said that his parents are just making everything up, and the people at the abductee group seemed weird, Dad. Like, the whole festival just seemed... I don't know...

Seemed what?

Perfect.

What's wrong?

Ruby just blew something. Ahh. I don't have any more coolant! Dang it!

What does this mean? Are we gonna miss it?

Do you have any cell service out here?

No.

I think there's a gas station just down the road. I think we have to push the car.

Wait, what?

Can you go around the back and push on the bumper? I'll push and steer.

Nice and easy.

HOOOWL

Hey there.

Hi. I was wondering if anyone was around who might have a look at my car?

Sure. Buck is around here somewhere.

BUCK!

How can I help you folks?

So, our car broke down. We were able to push it here, but I can't get it to start at all.

Do you have an idea of what's wrong with it?

176

No, we were just driving down the road, and it seized up and died.

It keeps overheating, so we can't run the air-conditioning.

Yeah, I have to top it off with coolant sometimes.

Well, let's go have a look.

You and your dad been at the festival?

Ummm...Yeah.

I went a few years back. Just to see what all the hubbub was about, ya know?

Seemed like a bunch of nutters to me. My grandpa lived out here when that whole alien spaceship thing happened, ya know?

Really?

Oh yeah, and let me tell you, anytime anyone even mentioned little green men, he lost it. Thought it was the biggest crock of horse poop he'd ever heard.

What about, like, all the witnesses and stuff?

My grandpa knew some of the boys out at the air force base. Told him it was just some crash test dummies and a secret weather balloon meant to spy on the Russians. Got blown out of proportion.

I guess I can't complain too much, though. We get all you lookie-loos in here keeping our little town afloat.

Now, what's happened is your engine's overheated 'cause you got a nasty clog in your radiator hose.

How long you been driving it like this?

I don't know, maybe six months? Kept putting it off.

Not good.

Is it fixable? We have somewhere important to be, and we are already late.

In the middle of the desert at 10:00 p.m.?

We are looking for a UFO.

Right.

Well, now that we've flushed out the hose, you just need to fill 'er up with some new coolant and you can be on your way. But I recommend when you get home to get a new hose. Letting it go like that probably did some damage.

Thanks. I appreciate the help.

You gonna pay for that keychain?

Hey!

Good luck with the little green men.

We're here.

Are you coming?

No.

OK.

I think you are brave.

Thank you, Mr. Bell.
I think I've reached the point where it doesn't matter anymore what people say about me. I need to tell my story for my own peace of mind.

I can't give anyone proof of what I saw that night. I can't make anyone believe me, but maybe someone out there will, and they will feel a little less alone.

Come on. Let's go...

Dad! Wait!

No. I'm done waiting.

No, Dad. Look!

Maybe I was wrong. I thought the mountains were to the left of me in the vision, but maybe not.

Maybe we needed to be on the other side of them.

Maybe I was wrong about where Zeta Reticuli needed to be in the sky. Maybe this wasn't even the right meteor shower.

Maybe.

The Zeta Reticuli system only appears in the southern hemisphere, but by the time the meteor shower started, it would have dipped below the horizon. So maybe I really was wrong.

There must be another meteor shower.

What's that?

A souvenir.

I got you something, too. Open up the glove box.

Magical Mystery Tour!

They had it sitting at the counter when I went to pay for gas this morning. It's like it was meant to be.

Julia?

Yeah?

I'm sorry we didn't see them.

Me too.

I know they are out there.

ROSWELL, NM

Is this where you said Josh's family would be?

Looks like the place.

Hello, you two! Come take a seat!

Thank you.

You look tired. Were you up all night? Did they come?

No.

Oh, David, I'm so sorry.

Where's Josh?

He's in the back there, playing a game.

I'm gonna go say hi.

Me too. I just wanted him to be right so bad.

Maybe that's silly.

It's not silly.

My parents are so sure about it. It's their whole lives. It'd be nice if they were actually right.

Yeah. My dad gave up everything for this, and even though they didn't come, he still thinks it's true.

It just sucks that our parents are like this, ya know?

Sometimes I wish I could believe, too. It would make everything so much easier.

I don't know that believing is always easy.

In a way, I think they're kinda brave.

Brave?

Yeah. I mean everyone thinks they're crazy, but they don't care.

All I do is care what people think about me.

Even me?

This is chalcedony! It's, like, super rare!

You can keep it if you want. I'm a little disappointed to hear it's not from space.

BZZT

Sara

Is that your friend? The one in Hawaii?

Yeah.

Looks kinda boring.

Kids! Food's here!

So, Greg is telling me that next year Sig Bell is coming! What do you think?

Duh! We have to come!

What do you think, Josh?

Could be cool.

221

Acknowledgments

First, I'd like to thank my weird, wonderful, eccentric, amazing family—my mom, Melanie; my dad, Jason; and my brother, Jack. I definitely wouldn't have the career I have without all the love and support you've given me over my entire life. Thank you, Mom, for reading every draft of this book and assuring me it was good and that no one was going to fire me for all the misspelled words. You are an amazing writer and storyteller, and your advice always makes everything I do better. Plus, you put up with my sass, and for that, you are a saint.

I'd like to thank my sweet, funny friends Clive and Jonathan, who helped me make this book by giving me really helpful edits, like "This part is bad" and "Why did you do this part so bad?" Okay, that's just what I hear in my head when you tell me it isn't perfect. In reality, you guys always make my work better with incredibly smart and insightful comments. You guys are the best.

My generous, wonderful friends Michele and Glenn have put up with my baloney for many years and somehow still like having me around. You both inspire me to step out of my comfort zone and have new experiences that shape my storytelling for the better. You even put up with all my worries, like "What if I fall off a cliff?" or "What if that cute dog falls off a cliff?"

My loving grandparents, Linda, Carl, and Janet, who always hung up my weird childhood drawings like they were masterpieces, even that one where the mermaid had some really big seashells, if you know what I mean.

My dear friend and mentor Rilla, who helped me get my start. Your joy and enthusiasm for storytelling and characters have been so inspiring to me. I'm still always trying to get an A from you on every project I do.

My agent, Alex, who is always there, ready to write the emails I really don't want to write. You are so kind and amazing. Thank you so much for believing in this book and helping it find its way to Little, Brown Books for Young Readers.

The wonderful people at Little, Brown, but especially my editor, Andrea. Working with you has been a dream. You really helped me make this book exactly what I wanted it to be, and you didn't even call me out for the millions of grammatical mistakes.

I'd also like to thank Lonnie, Carissa, Kelsey, Maria, Lara, Brandy, Jamie, Dayna, Evony, Nate, Colton, and Honeydew for being such an amazing support system.

Lastly, thank you to the History channel for playing marathons of questionable UFO TV shows while I was growing up. I never would have written this book without you.

Seaerra Miller

Seaerra Miller grew up in a small town in Wyoming, where she spent her days picking dandelions and watching old Westerns from her grandma's small movie collection. In 2015, she moved to Portland, Oregon, to study art at the Pacific Northwest College of Art. Since graduating in the spring of 2017, she has worked for several publications and organizations, such as Cricket Media, Apartment Therapy, Oni Press, and Snapchat. She is now working with Flying Eye Books to create her own comics series and illustrate companion novels for the *Hilda* series on Netflix. Her work is often narrative, whimsical, and aimed toward kids, with bold color palettes and unique characters.